First published in North America by Good Books (2004), Intercourse, PA 17534

International Standard Book Number: 1-56148-430-X

Devised and produced by Tucker Slingsby Ltd,
Roebuck House, 288 Upper Richmond Road West,
London SW14 7JG, England

With thanks to Jane Scarsbrook for additional ideas

Printed in Singapore

Color reproduction by Bright Arts Graphics, Singapore

Bear in the Barnyard

Sue Robinson
Illustrated by Tony Morris

Good Books

Intercourse, PA 17534

Teddy Bear liked playing with the toy farm when everyone was asleep. He put the little cows and sheep in the field. He made sure the horse had a bucket of water and some hay to eat. He sat the chickens neatly on their nests and put the ducks in the pond.

One evening, when Teddy Bear was playing with the farm, he heard someone coming. He quickly jumped back into bed and closed his eyes.

There was a thud. Something heavy landed on the end of the bed. Bear opened one eye. It was a suitcase.

"Don't forget your boots," he heard a voice call. "It will be muddy on the farm."

"I want to see a real farm!" said Bear to himself as the door closed.

Bear grabbed his backpack and quickly packed everything he thought he might need.

He put in his blue boots, a clean hankie and his little plaid picnic blanket.

Then he hopped into the suitcase and snuggled down on some soft, woolly socks in the corner. Soon Bear was fast asleep.

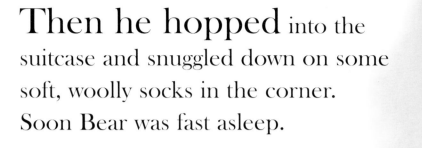

When he woke up, Bear peeped out of the suitcase. It was morning and he was alone in a strange room.

"I must be in the farmhouse!" he said to himself. "I can't wait to play with all the little farm animals!"

Bear hurried to the window and looked out. He could see the farmyard and the fields full of animals. It looked just like the toy farm at home!

He grabbed his backpack and rushed downstairs and out into the yard.

"**I'll say hello** to the horse first," said Bear
as he ran across the yard towards the stable. Inside
the stable it was dark. Bear peered at the ground.
He didn't want to step on the little horse!

Bear nearly jumped out of his furry skin when
a huge head appeared in front of him.

"Hrrrmph!" A big blast of air knocked Bear right over.
"Sorry," said the horse, "I thought you were a chicken.
They hide in here to lay their eggs sometimes."

"I'm not a chicken, I'm a teddy bear," whispered
Bear looking up at the huge horse.

"What do you do then?" asked the horse. "Do you lay
eggs or make milk? You are too small to pull a cart!"

"I'm a toy, I don't *do* anything," Bear replied.

"Hrrrmph," said the horse, tossing his head. "Teddy bears don't sound like they're of much use to me. All of us farm animals work hard and help the farmer. Climb onto my back. We must be able to find *something* useful you can do."

Bear climbed up and they set off across the farm. He was scared at first. The ground looked so very far away. But soon he began to enjoy himself. He felt very important on the big horse.

In fact, Bear began to feel quite brave.
"This is fun!" he thought, waving to a little bird.

"Perhaps you are a
sort of sheep," said the horse.
"You do have a woolly kind of coat."

And at that he tipped his head so Bear
slid off his back. And the horse cantered
away, leaving Bear in a field full of sheep.

Bear looked at the sheep. "Hello, I'm Teddy Bear," he said, feeling a bit shy.

"Beaaaar, Beaaar," echoed the sheep.

"You're very white and woolly," said Bear, picking bits of sheep's wool off his coat. "I'm going a bit bald on my elbows," he confided.

"Baaald, Baaaald," echoed the sheep.

"Oh dear, sheep are hard to talk to," thought Bear.

He took his boots from his backpack, tugged them on, and set off across the muddy field, still picking bits of sheep's wool off his fur.

"Who are you and where do you think you're going?" barked a loud voice. Bear jumped. He was nose to nose with a real, live, very cross-looking sheepdog.

"I'm Teddy Bear," said Bear in his bravest voice.

"Rrruff, I thought you were a rrrunaway sheep. What's that funny looking wool you're wearing?" asked the sheepdog.

"It's fur, not wool," said Bear proudly. "And I'm not a sheep. I think they're a bit silly."

"Of course they are," said the sheepdog. "That's why they need me to look after them. And I've got work to do." With a loud bark, the sheepdog bounded away.

Bear scrambled under a gate into the next field. It was muddy and a bit smelly.

"Ugh," said Bear, hopping out of the way of an enormous cow pie. "It's a good thing I remembered to bring my boots."

"Mooo, booots, what are they?" asked a deep voice.

Bear fell straight back into the cow pie. Looking up, he saw a long, large black and white nose. "Boots keep my feet clean," Bear said to the nose.
"I know," he went on, "you must be a cow. You give the farmer milk."

"Of course I'm a cow," said the cow. "What do you do?"

"I'm a teddy bear," said Bear. "And I have no job and everything here is just so-ooo-oo big."

Feeling very forlorn,
Bear started walking back towards
the farmyard.

"Talk to the chickens," the kind
cow mooed after him. "They
are about your size. Maybe
they can find you a job."

Bear wiped his hands and face with his clean hankie. Then he hurried off to find the chickens.

In the yard he followed the loud clucking noises into the henhouse. Inside it was warm and cozy. Bear could see rows of white and brown hens sitting on their straw nests. He tiptoed closer.

"Can you give me a job?" Bear asked a big
brown hen with a friendly face.

"You can look after my eggs for me," she said.
"I'd like to go out to stretch my legs
and find some food."

Bear was very happy. At last he
had something useful to do!

Bear wriggled and wiggled and jiggled but he couldn't stay comfortable for long. His bottom just wasn't big enough to cover all the eggs. He tried lying on his tummy and lying on his back.

Suddenly there was a loud CRACK!

Bear almost jumped out of his furry skin. He had broken one of the eggs!

He hopped off the eggs, just in time to see a little chick hatching from its egg. Soon there were more cracking noises, and more chicks appeared.

"I'd better find their mom," said Bear to himself as he set off with the little chicks cheeping behind him.

The happy hen clucked and fussed when she saw her chicks. She forgot all about Bear.

But just then a brightly colored bird strutted over. "How do you cock-a-doodle-do?" said the rooster, shaking Bear's paw with his wing.

Bear told the rooster everything that had happened.

"Well, I could use some help waking people up around here," the rooster said. "Show me what you can do."

Teddy Bear tried his very best cock-a-doodle-do. But his teddy growl just wasn't loud enough.

The rooster laughed and stalked away to cock-a-doodle-do on his own.

Bear sat down at the edge of the pond feeling very small and grubby. "I'm so covered in mud and wool and feathers I don't even look like a teddy bear. I'm not even good for cuddling now!"

"Quack, quack, come for a splash," cried the ducks, trying to cheer him up.

"Well, at least I *can* do that," smiled Bear, wading into the water.

Soon Bear's fur was washed clean. He pulled his plaid blanket from his backpack and dried himself, rubbing his fur until it was soft and fluffy. He felt like a brand new, huggable teddy bear again.

Bear smiled to himself. Suddenly he had a pretty good idea what his job was.

"And it's not here in the farmyard," he said to no one in particular.

Teddy Bear hurried into the farmhouse and crept back into the suitcase.

"I've found him," shouted a familiar voice. "He was here all along. That was lucky, Mommy. I would never have been able to sleep without Bear."

Bear smiled even more. Of all the jobs he could think of, he had the very best one.